Don Quixote

Retold and Illustrated by

Marcia Williams

WALKER BOOKS
LONDON

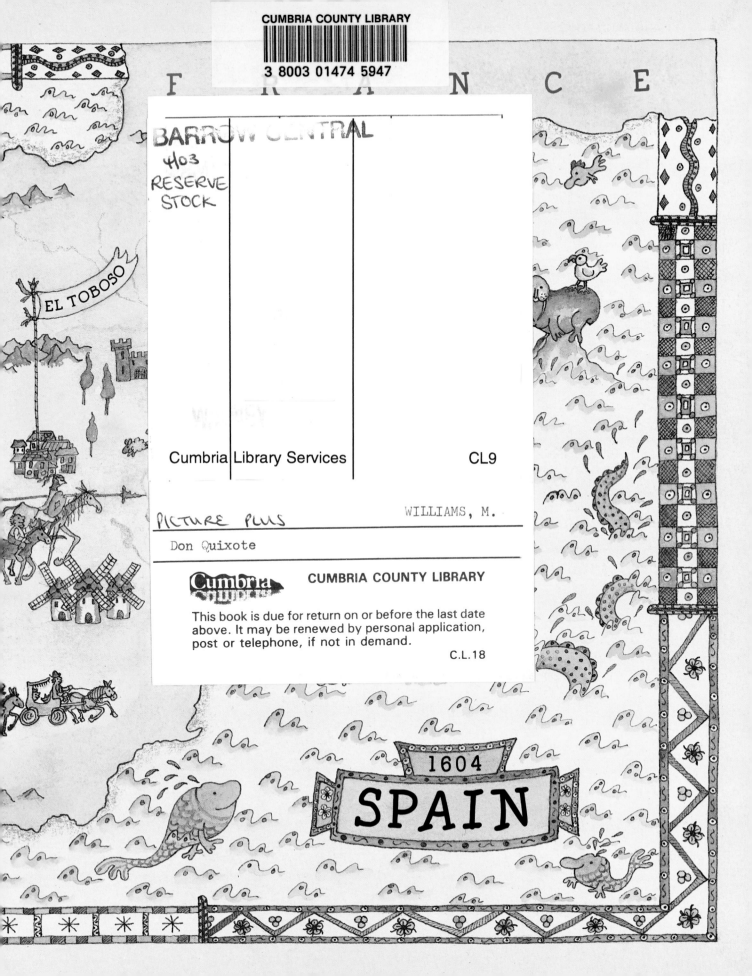

F R A N C E

EL TOBOSO

1604

SPAIN

Jenny Mike Amelia Sophie

First published 1993 by
Walker Books Ltd
87 Vauxhall Walk
London SE11 5HJ

© 1993 Marcia Williams

Printed and bound in Hong Kong by
South China Printing Co. (1988) Ltd

British Library Cataloguing in Publication Data
A catalogue record for this book is
available from the British Library.

ISBN 0-7445-2502-0

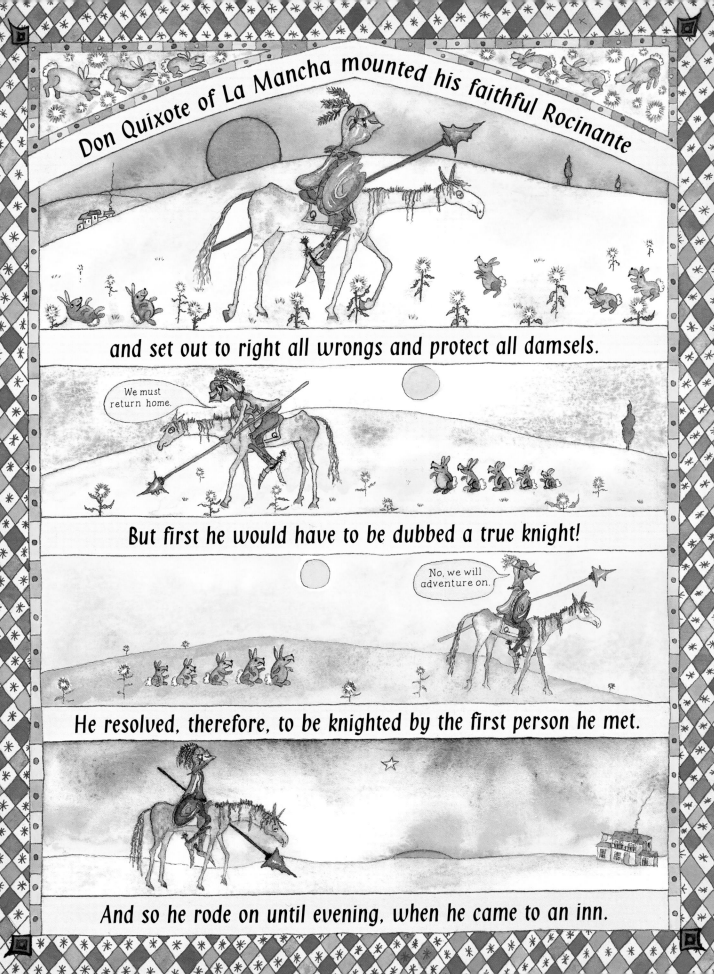

Now, to the eccentric Don Quixote the inn was a castle

and the innkeeper and travellers fine lords and ladies.

To them, Don Quixote was a madman, but they made him welcome

and the innkeeper agreed to dub him a "true" knight

if he could guard his armour until morning.

Putting his armour on a water trough, Quixote marched before it.

All went well until a carrier came to get water for his mules.

Furious at the disturbance, Don Quixote knocked the man unconscious

and moments later broke another carrier's head in four places.

The other travellers, woken by the noise, began to stone him.

The innkeeper soon stopped the shower of stones,

but he was anxious to be rid of his unusual guest.

So, with a brief ceremony, he pretended to knight Don Quixote,

and advised him to return home to La Mancha to fetch

some money, clean shirts, ointments and a squire to carry them.

He had not gone far when he met a group of merchants whom he

challenged to declare his Dulcinea the fairest Lady in the world.

When they refused, Don Quixote raised his lance and charged;

but Rocinante fell and it was the knight who was sorely beaten.

But where Don Quixote saw giants, Sancho saw windmills!
As Quixote charged towards them, the wind rose and
when he struck the nearest sail it turned with such force that
his lance broke, flinging both horse and rider to the ground.

The squire, protecting himself with a cushion,

gave Don Quixote a mighty blow,

which sliced off his visor and half his ear.

O vile scum!

Quixote, angered beyond reason,

sent mule and squire reeling.

Off with your head!

He would have cut off the squire's head

Great Knight, please pardon him.

He shall go at once to Dulcinea.

There, there. It's all over now.

if the lady had not pleaded for his life.

She promised to take the squire

to Dulcinea for his punishment.

Your poor ear.

This is a great dishonour.

Did we win an isle?

Heartbroken by his damaged helmet,

Quixote swore not to eat bread at table

until he had won a helmet just as fine.

Battered and weary, Don Quixote and Sancho Panza

spent the night with a group of astonished goatherds,

riding on next morning until they reached a stream.

Rocinante wandered over to some grazing mares,

but the unfriendly animals kicked and bit him.

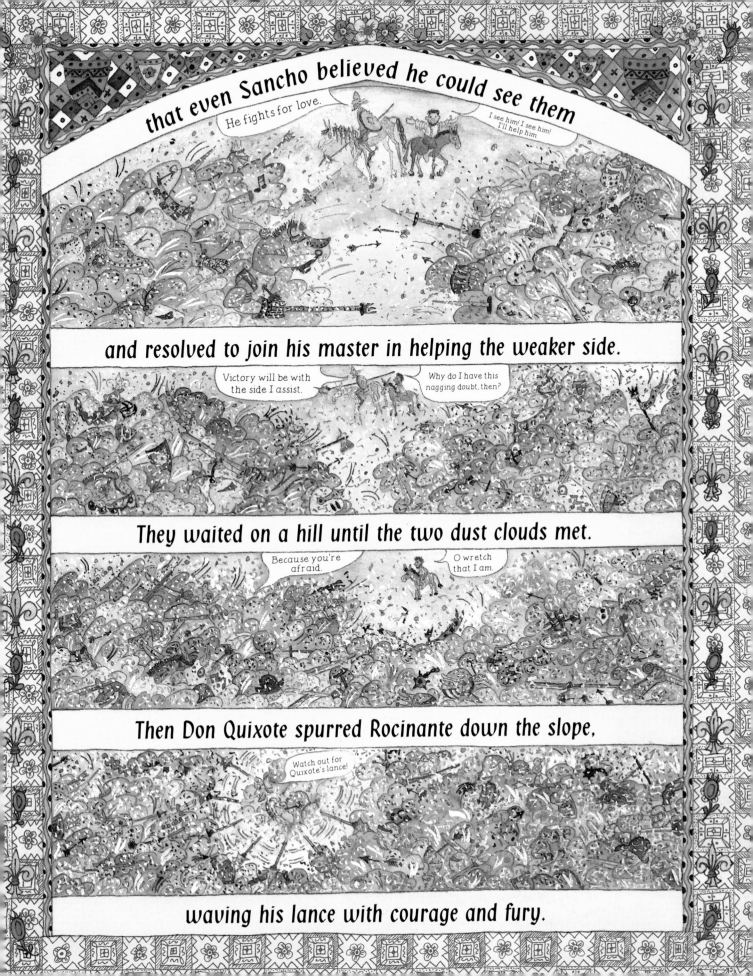

that even Sancho believed he could see them

and resolved to join his master in helping the weaker side.

They waited on a hill until the two dust clouds met.

Then Don Quixote spurred Rocinante down the slope,

waving his lance with courage and fury.

that the "armies" were flocks of sheep.
The shepherds yelled at Don Quixote and
threw stones, but Quixote's mind was with
knights of old and he continued his imaginary battle.

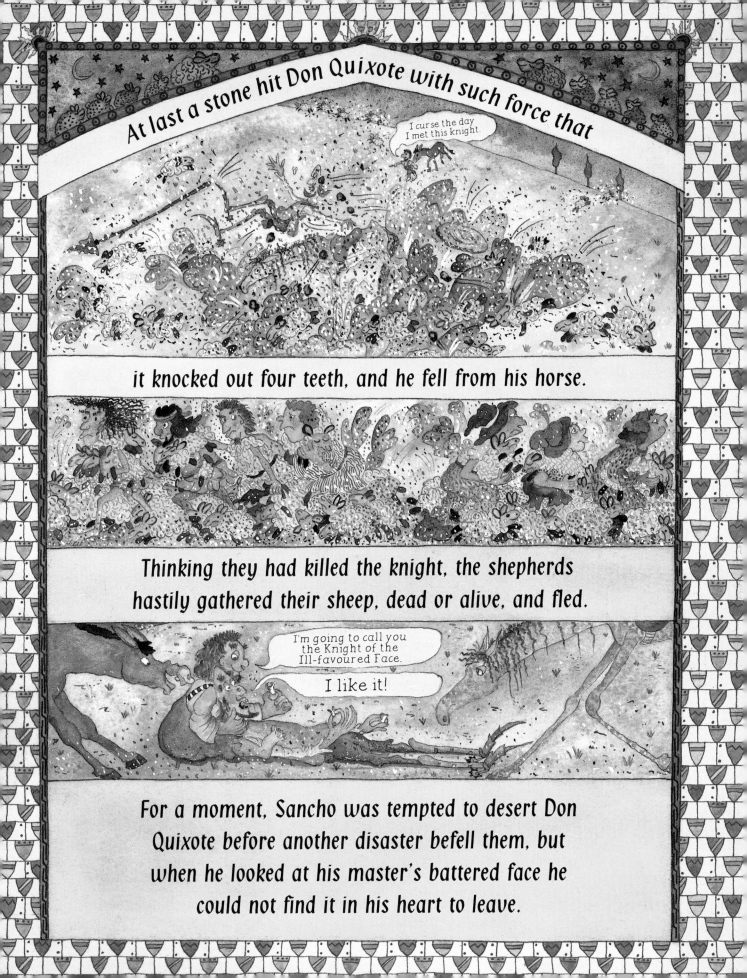

PORTUGAL

LA MANCHA